This edition published by Parragon Books Ltd in 2016

Parragon Books Ltd
Chartist House
15–17 Trim Street
Bath BA1 1HA, UK
www.parragon.com

Based on the screenplay *Pups and the Kitty-tastrophe*
Written by Ursula Ziegler Sullivan
Illustrated by Fabrizio Petrossi

ISBN 978-1-4748-3681-4

T#472240

Printed in China

ITTY-BITTY KITTY RESCUE

PaRragon

Bath • New York • Cologne • Melbourne • Delhi
Hong Kong • Shenzhen • Singapore

It was a warm, sunny day. Chase and Rubble were having a great time playing catch at the beach, when suddenly, they heard a far-off cry.

"Meow! Meow!"

A kitten was clinging to a toy boat out on the water! "Uh-oh!" Rubble cried. "That little kitty is in trouble." "We need to tell Ryder," Chase said.

Chase and Rubble raced to the Lookout
to tell Ryder about the kitty.
"No job is too big, no pup is too small!"
declared Ryder. He pushed a button on his
PupPad and sounded the PAW Patrol Alarm.

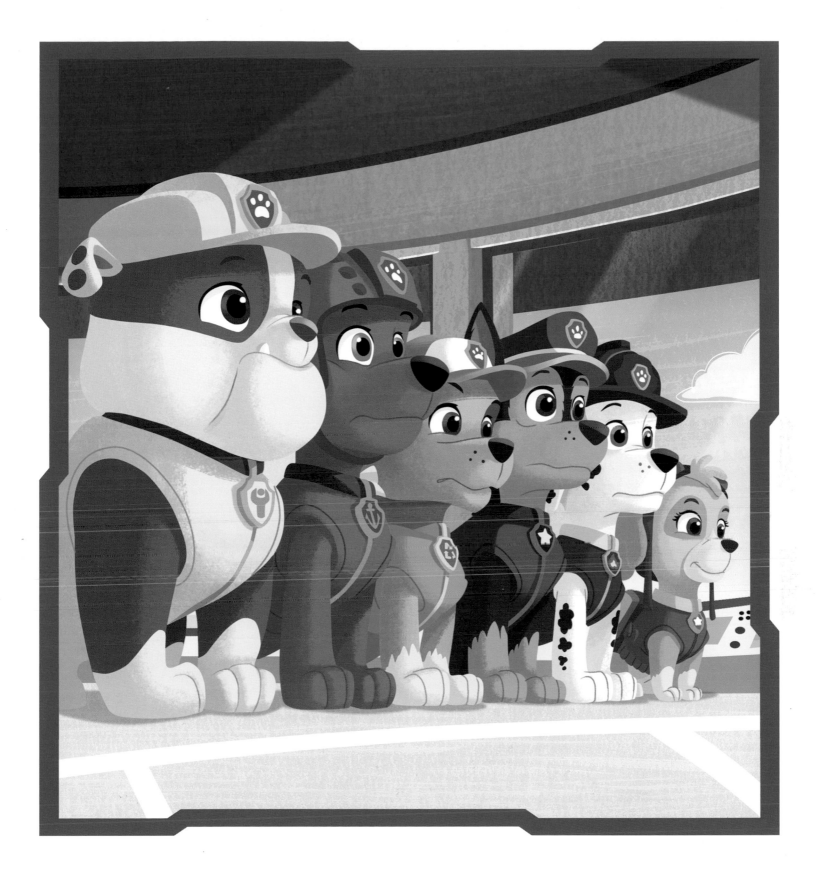

Minutes later, Marshall, Skye, Rocky and
Zuma joined their puppy pals at the Lookout.
"PAW Patrol is ready for action!" reported
Chase, sitting to attention.

"A kitten is floating out to sea," Ryder announced, pointing to the viewing screen behind him.
"We have to save the itty-bitty kitty!" Rubble exclaimed. Then he straightened up and added, "I mean, ahem, we have to save the kitten."

"Zuma, your hovercraft is perfect for a water rescue," Ryder said.

"Ready, set, get wet!" Zuma barked.

"And Skye," Ryder continued, "I'll need you and your helicopter to help find the kitten quickly."

"This pup's got to fly!" called Skye.

Zuma's hovercraft splashed across Adventure Bay.
Ryder turned his all-terrain-vehicle into a jet-ski
and followed. Up above, Skye zoomed through the air.
Soon, she spotted the little kitten in the water below.
  "We're here to help you," Ryder told the kitten,
easing his jet-ski to a stop.

But the little kitten jumped from her boat and landed right on Zuma's head. Then the startled pup fell out of the hovercraft and into the water!

Zuma yelled, "Don't touch the –"

ZOOM! The kitten accidentally hit the throttle and raced off on the hovercraft.

The hovercraft zoomed around the bay.
Up above, Skye turned this way and that,
trying to follow the hovercraft's twisting course.
"This kitty is making me dizzy," she groaned.

Ryder pulled up next to the hovercraft and jumped on board. He stopped the engine and gently picked up the shivering kitten.

"Everything's all right," he said, pulling a slimy piece of seaweed off the kitten. "Let's take you back to dry land and get you cleaned up."

Later that day, Rubble skateboarded into Katie's Pet Parlour with his new best friend. "Aw, whose cute kitty is that?" Katie asked. "I don't know," Rubble explained. "We found her on the bay with no collar or tags, just this purple ribbon."

"Does the kitty-widdy
want a nice warm bath?"
Rubble asked.
    "*Meow,*" the kitten replied.
    "Do you want me to do it?" Katie asked.
"Cats can be a little tricky to bathe."
    "Tricky?" Rubble said. "Not this little sweetie."

But the kitten had other ideas. The moment she touched the water, she jumped away with a screech.

The kitten scurried along shelves, splashing water and knocking over bottles of shampoo.

Rubble slipped on a spinning bottle ...

... then the kitten fell onto Rubble's skateboard and rolled out of the door!

Down the street from Katie's Pet Parlour, Ryder got a message from Rocky: ***"A little girl is looking for her lost kitty called Precious."***
   Ryder recognized the kitten in the picture the girl was holding. Before Ryder could say a word, Precious rolled past on Rubble's skateboard! She skated down a hill and disappeared into town.

"Chase, it's time to use your Super Sniffer!"
Ryder said.
    Chase needed something with the kitty's
scent on it. Luckily, they had her purple ribbon.
    Chase took a deep sniff. "She went that way –
ACHOO! Sorry. Cat hair makes me sneeze."

Sniff, sniff, sniff.
Chase followed the scent until he found Rubble's skateboard at the bottom of the town hall steps. "Good sniffing, Chase!" Ryder said.

Ryder and the pups looked around and saw
a shocking sight.
The kitty was inside the town hall's bell tower!
Ryder pulled out his PupPad and called for
Marshall and his fire truck.

"I'm all fired up!" Marshall said as his fire truck screeched to a halt in front of the town hall. Just then, the little kitten's owner arrived, too!

Ryder told Marshall to put up his ladder.
"We need to get the kitten down from that tower."
"I'm on it!" called Marshall. He extended the
truck's ladder and carefully started to climb.

Marshall reached the top of the ladder.
The scared little kitten was clinging
desperately to a rope in the tower.
"Don't worry," Marshall said softly.
"I'll get you down safely. Come here."
"Meow," Precious whimpered.

The kitten jumped from the rope. She tried to grab Marshall's helmet but missed – and clutched his face instead!

"Whoa!" Marshall yelped. He couldn't see a thing! The ladder shook and Marshall lost his grip. Then he and the kitten fell off the ladder!

But Ryder caught Marshall, and the little kitty tumbled straight into her owner's arms!

"Precious!" the girl exclaimed. "I'm so glad you're okay! You owe these brave pups a thank you for all their help."

"Whenever you need us," Ryder said, "just yelp for help!"

The End

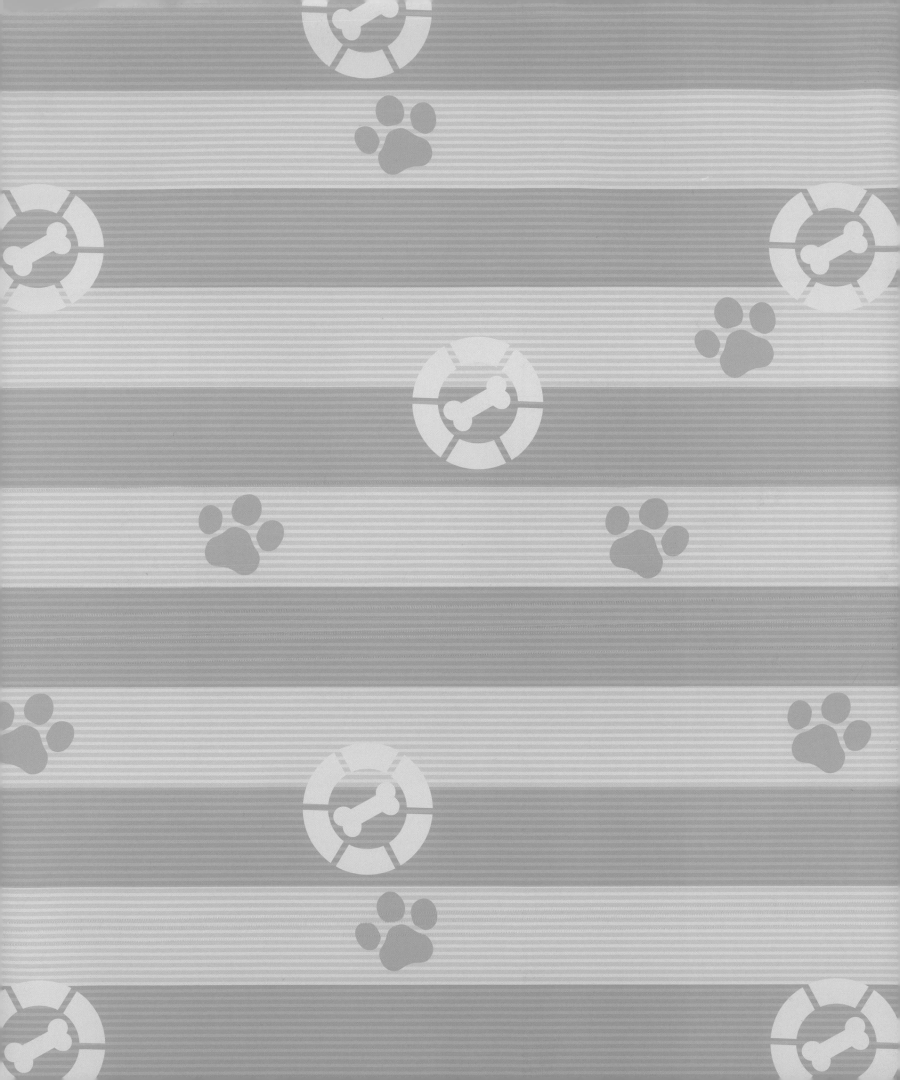